TEDDY B

The Rev Patrick Ashe is a retired vicar who has worked for many years for the cause of children, having been a chaplain for youth and the founder of two relief organisations: Project Vietnam Orphans and Christian Outreach. He has seven children who were the first to hear these stories before they were written down for a wider audience.

By the same author:
Teddy Brown Finds a Home
Teddy Brown is Rescued
Teddy Brown's Secret
Teddy Brown and the Battle
Teddy Brown Goes on Holiday
Teddy Brown and the Aeroplane
Teddy Brown Puts the World Right

Teddy Brown
Helps Jack

PAT ASHE

KINGSWAY PUBLICATIONS
EASTBOURNE

Text illustrations and cover design by John Dillow

British Library Cataloguing in Publication Data

Ashe, Pat
Teddy Brown helps Jack.
I. Title   II. Series
823'.914 [J]

ISBN 0-86065-785-X

Printed in Great Britain for
KINGSWAY PUBLICATIONS LTD
1 St Anne's Road, Eastbourne, E Sussex BN21 3UN by
Stanley L. Hunt (Printers) Ltd, Rushden, Northants.
Typeset by Nuprint Ltd, Harpenden, Herts

For Robert
and all the children who listen
to these stories

Contents

A WORD TO
PARENTS AND TEACHERS

In this eighth book about Teddy Brown, children may learn the danger of being pressurised by their peers into doing what they know is wrong, and that having God's love in their hearts is more important than keeping a set of rules.

At the end of the book there are suggested Bible readings if you should want to get children used to handling a Bible. I recommend using a modern translation such as J. B. Phillips or *The Living Bible*.

1

TIGER TRICKS
THE KNAVE OF HEARTS

Poor Jack, the Knave of Hearts, found it very difficult to get rid of his old nature, and once again he began to fall back into his old ways. When he first asked Jesus to take over his life, some of the other toys said, 'Ha! It won't last long. Knave of Hearts will never change—you wait and see!'

And of course you may remember he did have that trouble with Elephant's doughnuts.*

After that, he really changed. He was

---

* See Book 4.

happy, and sang, and went around with Giraffe, Pink Rabbit and Teddy Brown, and they used to read the Bible, and say their prayers with Robby, and go to church with him. Some of the other toys watched Knave, and every time he did something they thought was not Christian, they jumped on him. It was the Black-and-white Tiger who was the worst. He seemed really cross that Knave had become a Christian.

Tiger went round telling all the others how good *he* was. He never did anyone any harm, he said. He did bite people's heads off now and then, but after all—that was only to be expected. It was his nature—he was a tiger.

Tiger was always on about Knave of Hearts. He tried every way to make the other toys dislike him. He spread stories about him which were not true. He even took things and accused Knave of having done it. But nothing seemed to upset Jack, the Knave of Hearts.

Then Teddy Brown began to notice that

Jack always seemed to have an excuse for not going to church with them. He mentioned it to Pink Rabbit.

She said, 'Come to think of it, I haven't seen him reading his Bible lately. I hope he is not forgetting to pray.'

Teddy Brown had a word with Jack, but he said, 'Oh, I don't need all that stuff. I find I can get on quite all right without it.'

Tiger got crosser and crosser with Knave. One day he bit him, and Jack went to Teddy Brown and Pink Rabbit to have a patch sewn on. He said, 'Poor Tiger, he is really savage about us being Christians. He must have a very guilty conscience.' Then he went on, 'But Tiger is stupid really, and if I wanted to I could soon put him in his place.'

Teddy Brown felt uneasy. It was a bit like the old swaggering, crafty Knave speaking. He said, 'You'd better keep close to Jesus, Jack, or the devil will get at you.'

'Oh well, I haven't done too badly so far, you must admit. I've done all the things Jesus said.'

As he went off, Teddy Brown said to Pink Rabbit, 'I hope Jack is going to be all right. Robby says, "Pride comes before a fall." '

Now, of course Tiger knew that Jack the Knave of Hearts adored tarts, and he knew that at one time Jack just could not resist them.

One afternoon Mummy had been baking some. She said to Tiger, 'Tiger, would you look after the tarts while I go down to the shops? I don't want the dog to get them while they're cooling.'

Tiger said he would.

After she had gone, he had an idea. He called the Knave of Hearts. 'You wouldn't do something for me, would you?'

'Oh yes, I would,' said Jack. 'I'm a Christian—I'll do you a good turn.'

'Then will you look after the tarts till Mummy gets back?'

'Yes, all right,' said Jack.

Tiger went off and hid.

The smell of those tarts! It made Jack's mouth water. He went and looked at them.

They looked the best tarts Mummy had ever made. 'I bet they'd melt in my mouth,' he thought.

Tiger came up behind him and whispered in his ear. 'They're lovely, aren't they—enough to make your mouth water. Why don't you have one?'

'No,' said Knave of Hearts.

'Go on, no one will know. Even Mummy won't notice just one!'

'No,' said Knave of Hearts.

'You're afraid, that's why.'

'I'm not afraid of anything,' said Jack boldly.

'Well, have one and let's see.'

'No, I don't want one.'

'There you are. I told you—you're scared. You're just a cissy. You're frightened.'

'I'm not.'

'Well, take one and prove it.'

And although a little voice was saying to Jack, 'Don't touch it,' he put out his hand and took one, and started to eat it—just to show Tiger he was not frightened.

And you should have seen the smile on the Tiger! He looked like a Cheshire cat.

While Knave was munching the tart, they heard the key in the front door. It was Mummy. Knave ran off and hid. He felt terribly ashamed—he did not want to see her.

Tiger said, 'That knave has been at your tarts. He's behind the toy cupboard eating one.'

'Jack,' said Mummy, 'where are you?'

No answer.

'Jack, what have you been doing?'

No answer.

Later on Teddy Brown found Jack looking miserable. 'Oh, Teddy Brown,' he said, 'I've been a knave again. I've let Jesus down. I've let you all down. I'm not fit to be called a Christian. I wish I was dead.' And he began to cry.

'You're sorry, aren't you, Jack?' said Teddy Brown.

'Oh yes, I'm sorry—terribly sorry, but what good is that? I can't un-eat the tart. I've stolen again. I'm a thief. I'm as bad as I ever was.'

'I know how you feel,' said Teddy Brown, 'because I've felt like that. But I know something else too. I know it can all be put right.'

'Oh, I don't think it can, because I knew I was doing wrong. I knew Jesus was saying,

15

"Don't do it," but I listened to Tiger, and took the tart just to prove I was not afraid.'

'If you say sorry to Jesus he will forgive you. It says in the Bible that there is no sin he won't forgive if we are really sorry.'

'But is that enough,' asked Jack, 'just to tell him I'm sorry?'

'No, not quite enough. You can't earn his forgiveness, nor deserve it, but you can accept it.'

'Yes,' said Jack tearfully.

'And then you must go and say sorry to Mummy.'

So they knelt down, and Jack said he was sorry to Jesus—and he knew Jesus had forgiven him. And then he went and said sorry to Mummy, and she forgave him too. And it felt like a great load off his mind, and they were all happy again.

Except Tiger—he was furious.

So when you hear a little voice in your mind saying, 'Jesus would not do that,' then don't do it, because if you do, it will make you miserable.

But it is wonderful to know that he forgives us. So let us say sorry for anything we have done when we know Jesus said, 'Don't.'

'Lord Jesus, I'm sorry. Please make me strong to listen only to your voice.

'Amen.'

2

DUCK GETS HOOKED

A cousin of Robby's called Danny came to live with him for a while, and he brought with him a toy called Smart Alec. He wore a well-cut suit, and pointed shoes, and he went to live with the other toys in Robby's toy cupboard.

You may remember that when the pond ran dry, Duck had started smoking. When he tried to give it up, he got so irritable that one day Smart Alec said, 'Here, have one of my cigarettes. It will calm your nerves.'

So Duck took one, and it made him feel fine, but after a while he began to feel sad and miserable.

'Can I have another of your cigarettes, please Alec?'

So Alec gave him another, and then another, and each time Duck smoked one, he felt fine.

'Your cigarettes are really super,' Duck said to Smart Alec. 'Can I have some more?'

Alec said, 'Don't tell anyone, but these cigarettes have something special in them that makes you feel good.' Then he added, 'But they are rather expensive.'

Then the trouble started for poor Duck. He found he just could not do without them. After he had smoked one, he felt on top of the world, but not long after he felt terrible—depressed and irritable, and he started to tremble. He felt much worse than before.

He went to Alec for another one, but Alec said, 'Hey, you'd better start buying your own. I can get them for you if you like.'

When Duck heard the price, he nearly died. They were terribly expensive. So he decided to give them up.

Oh dear, it was easier to decide to stop smoking them than it was to do it. He felt such a longing for those cigarettes that he spent all his pocket-money on them.

When he had no more money, he said to Smart Alec, 'Oh Alec, I'm just longing for one of those cigarettes, but I'm absolutely broke. How do you manage to buy them?'

Alec's advice to Duck was very bad. He said, 'Well, when I run out of money, I just go and pinch some.'

Duck was shocked. 'You mean you steal?'

'Yes,' said Alec, cool as a cucumber. 'As a matter of fact, I've discovered where Danny keeps his pocket-money. He never notices when I've taken some. He keeps me in smokes, though he doesn't know it.'

Duck was horrified. He could hardly believe what Alec had said. 'You don't mean you steal from your best friend?'

'Well, have you got any better ideas?' Alec asked. 'I can show you where Robby keeps his money, if you like.'

'No,' said Duck. 'I'd never steal anything from Robby.'

'Please yourself,' said Alec with a shrug, 'but if you dare tell on me, I'll set fire to your tail.'

All the other toys noticed that there was something wrong with Duck. He looked awful. He never bothered to have a bath in the pond. His feathers were all droopy, his eyes looked funny; and he was shaky. Teddy Brown got him alone one day, and said, 'Duck, you don't look at all well. Don't you think you ought to see the doctor?'

But Duck said, 'No, no, no, I don't want to see a doctor.'

Teddy Brown consulted Robby, and Robby told Daddy about Duck, and Daddy said he would keep an eye on him for a few days. Then he said to Robby, 'You know, Robby, I think Duck's on drugs.'

Robby decided to tackle Duck about it. 'Duck,' he said, 'I know you started smoking when the pond ran dry, but are you smoking cigarettes with drugs in them?'

Duck was ashamed and terrified. He quickly decided to tell a lie. 'Of course not,' he said. 'What on earth can have given you that idea?'

But Robby knew that drugs not only made people ill—they also make them steal and tell lies.

'Duck,' he said, 'you need help.'

Duck began to cry. 'Oh Robby, I feel so miserable. I've tried to give it up, and I can't. I don't know what to do.'

Robby said, 'You're hooked, which means in your own strength you won't be able to give it up.'

'Oh, I wish I'd never started,' sobbed Duck. 'But they made me feel so much better, and I thought I could stop whenever I wanted—and now I find I can't.'

Robby said, 'There is only one way you can break free. We will get Teddy Brown, and Pink Rabbit, and Knave of Hearts to pray for you, and we must ask Jesus for his help.'

Duck asked Jesus to give him his Spirit and his strength so that he might be able to give up those terrible cigarettes. The other toys who had asked Jesus into their lives rallied round, and one of them always stayed near Duck. They encouraged him, and prayed with him, and whenever Duck wanted to smoke, they got him to think about Jesus until the longing passed. It was a terrible struggle for Duck, but little by little Jesus took away the longing until he was completely free.

But Smart Alec did not ask Jesus to help him. He went on smoking, and although he wanted to give up drugs, he just could not. In the end he got so dirty and rotten that Danny had to throw him into the dustbin. The rest of the toys were also very sad, because Alec had been so clean and smart when he first joined them. But that is what happens to those who cannot give up drugs, and do not ask Jesus for his help.

3

MISS GOODY-GOOD

Another new toy came to live in the toy cupboard. She was called Miss Goody-good. She was made all of cloth, had her hair done up in a bun, and had no paint on her face. She was very prim and proper.

Not long after she arrived, she got all the Christian toys together. She said, 'We must not have anything to do with the others—they are bad. We must keep away from Toy Soldier—he swears; and from Golden-haired Doll—she wears lipstick. Some even smoke, like Duck used to, and they don't say Grace.'

Pink Rabbit went pinker when she heard

that, because she sometimes forgot to say Grace.

Miss Goody-good went on and on, and the others nodded politely.

One day at lunch Pink Rabbit forgot to say her Grace. Miss Goody-good called them together. 'We can't have this sort of thing,' she said. Pink Rabbit didn't say her Grace. We must kick her out.'

Some of them nodded, but Teddy Brown wondered whether Jesus would really mind if Pink Rabbit forgot to say Grace.

A few days later, Miss Goody-good heard Giraffe singing a song that was not a hymn. She called them together. 'Giraffe was singing a pop song,' she said. 'We can't have him in our group.'

So poor Giraffe was excluded. She saw Teddy Brown shaking his head sadly, and she scowled at him.

Although Knave of Hearts had asked Jesus into his heart, Miss Goody-good was not convinced he was a real Christian because sometimes Knave did wrong things. But whenever that happened he felt so bad about hurting Jesus that he always said 'Sorry', and was so humble that the others forgave him.

One day Knave helped himself to three tarts. Miss Goody-good looked down her nose: 'Jesus doesn't like greedy people.'

That made Knave cross. He turned on her: 'Oh you're such a goody-goody, you never do anything wrong! How about for-giving people instead of always scowling at them?'

Miss Goody-good said it was time they threw Knave out. The ones who were left went around with long faces, afraid they might break one of Miss Goody-good's rules.

Teddy Brown said to her one day, 'I'm afraid you're so busy trying to be good that you have forgotten about loving people.'

That made her really angry, and she told Teddy Brown he was not fit to be in her group.

So one by one she threw them all out until she was left on her own. She went round with a scowl on her face, trying to look like a martyr.

But the ones she had thrown out were happy. They laughed and sang, and they loved each other and forgave each other when things went wrong. They said Grace, not because they had to, but because they wanted to thank Jesus for all he had done for them. They sang hymns, not because they were afraid of Miss Goody-good's scowl, but because they

wanted to praise God. They wanted to be like Jesus, not because they were afraid, but because they knew he loved them and they loved him, so they did not want to disobey him.

Miss Goody-good began to feel very lonely, and the more she saw how free and happy the others were, the lonelier she felt.

At last she went to Robby and said, 'I've tried to be a Christian and be good and keep all the rules, but it has not made me really happy. What do you think is wrong?'

Robby thought for a bit. Then he said, 'I think Jesus wants us to love him and each other as he loves us, and to forgive each other as he has forgiven us. So we need his love in our hearts.'

After that, Miss Goody-good began to change as she let the love of Jesus fill her heart. She told the others she was sorry she had set herself up as a judge. She became their friend, and was really happy.

Suggested Bible Readings

1. Tiger Tricks the Knave of Hearts

Genesis 3:1–13.

2. Duck Gets Hooked

1 Corinthians 10:12–13.

3. Miss Goody-good

John 1:16–17; 13:34–35.
Romans 8:38–39.
Galatians 2:16.